To our children Sophia,
Raphael, Clara, Karl,
Isabelle, Alexandra,
and Aida

May your lives be
stories full of magic,
wonder, family,
friendship, and love.

AIDA
AND THE
TREE OF MUSIC
Written by
Fouad Boulos and Samer Nassif

Illustrated by Anne Buguet
Edited by Luke Farmkiss

When Aida was a baby girl,
the Tree in the garden right
outside her bedroom window
would play beautiful music
and sing beautiful songs.

Every night when Aida went to
bed, her parents read her
bedtime stories, the Tree
played music, and Aida
listened until she fell asleep.

For years, Aida would not sleep without being cradled by the Tree's enchanting songs. Until one night, Aida tucked herself into bed and waited, but silence was all she heard.

"Tree, why aren't you singing?" Aida asked. The Tree did not answer.

Aida begged the Tree to play a tune, any tune, but the Tree remained silent; its leaves and roots were still. Aida could not sleep that night. She went into the garden under the moonlit sky, sat under the Tree, and started crying. Her eyes were sleepless, her heart was sad, and she missed the music deeply.

A Turtle with a golden shell was passing through the garden and saw Aida crying. "What's the matter young girl?" he asked with concern. She told him about the Tree and the music, and how it had all stopped.

"Find the Well of Stories," the Turtle said, "for it holds many secrets and might know what happened to the Tree. Seek the Whistling Fox who lives at the far end of the forest. Only he knows how to find the Well."

"Can you take me to the Fox at the far end of the forest?" asked Aida.

"I could," the Turtle said, "but I am slow and it would take so long that, by the time we get there, you would have forgotten about the Tree."

Aida walked by herself for a long time but could not find the Fox. Tired, she sat down in the shade and hummed the saddest song the forest had ever heard.

A Cardinal on a nearby branch was moved by Aida's singing and wanted to help her. "I can help you find the Fox," he whispered in her ear, "but the Fox hides from people, and he might not let you see him."

"But I must find him," Aida said. So Aida and the Cardinal traveled togther to the far end of the forest. The Cardinal told Aida to wait there quietly for the Fox. Then he flew away and Aida was once again alone.

Aida sat and waited for a long while, but she was so weary she fell asleep. Meanwhile, the Fox had been carefully watching her. Her sad little face touched his heart, but he was too frightened to come closer.

When Aida woke up, a voice in her heart told her she should not be quiet anymore. She started singing a song the Tree had sung to her many times before. It was a song about friends who were always there for one another. Soon after Aida began singing, the Fox started whistling along.

"You are the whistling Fox!" Aida said joyfully. "I need you to help me find the Well of Stories."

"The Well," the Fox said, "travels from one land to another gathering stories. It tells its stories to the Wind who carries them to the world."

"Learn this tune, close your eyes, believe, and whistle. The Wind will answer and take you to the Well." The Fox gave Aida the tune, then vanished into the woods.

Aida closed her eyes and whistled. The Wind whistled back, took Aida's hand and gently carried her to a far away land. After a long journey, the Wind and Aida stopped.

Aida opened her eyes to find an old brick well with a worn out empty wooden bucket and a frayed rope. She waited for the well to talk to her, but it did not. She peered into its depths, talked, whistled, sang, and even shouted, but all she heard was the echo of her own voice.

"Maybe the Well of Stories would like to hear my story first," Aida thought.

She sat down and started telling the Well about the day she was born, how the Tree of music lost its voice, and how she met the Turtle, the Cardinal, the Fox, and the Wind. As she spoke, a drop of water started whirling in the bucket, slowly filling it. As the bucket filled, Aida could hear water move in the depths of the Well as the Wind whistled between its walls.

Aida understood the Well was thanking her for her story by giving her water in the bucket to quench her thirst. As soon as she drank, the Well started telling its amazing tales...

...of the boy who traveled beyond the stars and saw the outer shape of space.

...of the cobbler on the mountain top who turned clouds into shoes for giants.

...of the flower that only bloomed after it rained drops of starlight.

...of vast lands of magical shells that danced on the beach sand.

...of the man with a heart so big he put everyone in it.

The stories filled Aida's heart with so much joy she felt she could fly. The Well then called the Wind to take her back home.

"But you did not tell me why the Tree stopped singing!" Aida shouted as the Wind carried her away.

"The answer is within you," answered the Well. "Just remember what makes your heart sing."

When Aida was back in her garden, she stood in front of the Tree. "My beautiful Tree, you will not believe what I have seen and heard. Let me tell you all about it!" she said with overwhelming excitement.

As the Tree listened to Aida's
stories, its branches started
moving again, its leaves and roots
started dancing, and the Tree
began making the beautiful music
that Aida had missed so much.

It was then that Aida understood
the Tree only sang to stories. She
remembered telling her parents
one night that she was too old for
bedtime stories. That was the
night the music stopped and her
incredible adventure began.

Every night since her adventure
ended, Aida would sit on her bed
with her parents and share all
sorts of stories, real, imaginary,
funny, bittersweet stories, and
stories about friends like the
Turtle, the Cardinal, the Fox, the
Wind, and the Well.

As the Tree listened to Aida and
her parents, it sang and played its
beautiful music until Aida rested
her head on her pillow and fell
asleep.

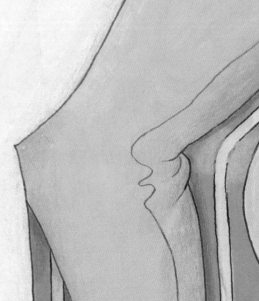

Printed in Great Britain
by Amazon